The Nature
and
Other Short Stories

Originally written in Tamil by
AR. Arul Selvan

Translated by
Meyyappan Devarajan

Edited by
Mohamed
TransCloud Language Services
Chennai

NOTION PRESS

NOTION PRESS

India. Singapore. Malaysia.

Published Year: 2025

To Father...

**(The person who encouraged me in
writing and now lives in my memories)**

Contents

1. BUD BECOMES FLOWER

Kannamma's troubles started as the textile mill where her husband worked was closed. A year has passed since they said that they would open it the next week.

It was only when the family started struggling for food that Kannamma started to earn money by working in the houses of big men at neighbourhood and sending her ten-year-old son to sell flowers in the evenings after school. Kannamma felt the pain of having to spoil the boy's studies, but she had no choice other than sending him to sell flowers.

Within this one year, her husband had become addicted to both drinking and card games. With much efforts she tried to stop it, that didn't work. "Negotiation wins" is often reported in the daily news. But the opening of the plant was going to be a daydream.

Kannamma went in search of her husband as he did not come home till late that day. The news of the person running opposite struck her like a thunderbolt. "Kannamma, your husband has been admitted to the hospital"

Kannamma's husband was one of those who had been admitted to the hospital after drinking poisonous liquor in the town. When she ran there, he was dead.

Kannamma fell ill with fever after spending all the money she had on her husband's funeral. Even though she was not feeling well, the women around her were busy removing her flower, forehead sticker and wedding chain.

"Why did you take the flower from mother"

The son asked the women next door.

"Your papa is dead....so she mustn't put flowers anymore..." they replied casually.

He hated the flower. He decided not to sell flowers anymore.

But -

Even after a week, Kannamma did not recover. He knew that there was no money in the house.

"I have to take my mother to the hospital and buy medicine. Then I need money for food..."

He thought.

"No more flowers to be sold" his zeal was shattered. He used to go to school and sell flowers in the evening, he stopped going to school and started working at a flower shop.

****

2. THE STUDY

Shanmuganathan told his son Maran with a smile of satisfaction.

"I have prepared thirty lakh rupees for your medical seat..."

Maran had completed his secondary education in school. But he did not get a place in the medical college as he scored few marks low in the entrance examination.

In order not to disappoint him, Shanmuganathan decided to admit him anyway in a private medical college. The position is that the place will be available only if thirty lakh rupees to be donated to college. Shanmuganathan had tried hard for a week to collect the rupees. That is what he happily told his son Maran.

Maran looked at his father with no temptation on his face. Maran's sight surprised Shanmuganathan.

"Are you happy..." he asked.

"Dad I have changed my decision to join medical college..." Shanmuganathan was stunned to hear this.

"What....what's the reason?"

"Just thinking about our family situation..."

"Can you think of all that if you want to study the doctor course?..."

"Yesterday, I thought carefully and decided. I am going to use the thirty lakh rupees in some other way..."

"What is your idea?"

"Today there is a good demand for plastic products in the market. I will buy plastic moulding machines for this rupees and start the business..."

Shanmuganathan thought for a few seconds. Then he happily patted him on the back.

****

3. DISAPPOINTMENT

"Bala....come here..." Panneerselvam called his son. "What?" Balan stood near him while tying his tie.

"I remembered an interesting incident that happened while I was at work. I called to tell you about it."

"Dad...I'm leaving urgently...I have an office inspection today. I'll hear about it on Sunday. Shall I start?..." He left the house.

Panneerselvam called "Shanti...Shanti..." "Uncle...here I come..." The daughter-in-law came running with a voice.

"What, Have all the work completed? Do you hear me telling an interesting thing that happened while I was working?"

"Sorry uncle...today is the anniversary of our women's association. The ceremony will start only after I reach there. We will talk one day restly uncle" Shanti left without waiting for an answer.

Panneerselvam retired from Railway Department. He feels that no one respect him after he retires. Accordingly, even today, his son and daughter-in-law left after dismissing what he had said, which made him sad.

"Grandpa...grandpa..." Grandson Karthi came running. "Come on Karthi...sit down. At least you listen to me..." Panneerselvam called him closer.

"Grandpa.. I am going to play cricket," he said and pointing to a boy who had come with him. "He is my friend's brother. His mother and father have gone shopping. They asked him to stay in our house till they come. I leave..." he said and ran away.

Panneerselvam started narrating to the boy all the events that had happened while he was at work, happy that he had come to listen to him. The boy was also listening all with a smile.

A few hours later, grandson Karthi came home after playing cricket.

"Grandpa...grandpa...his mother and father have come. They have asked to bring him home immediately." he said.

Panneerselvam said with a smile, "Karthi...you know what a good boy he is. He sat patiently and listened to everything I said. But...he doesn't want to say his name, even though he has been asked several times."

"How would he say grandpa. He can't hear. Can't even talk. Too pity he's dumb Grandpa..." Panneerselvam's head was spinning when Karthi said.

14

******

4. THE LEADER

Workers are gathered all over the room. Slogans such as "Labor Unity up up", "Sindabad, Sindabad Workers Unity Sindabad" "Never Lose, Never Lose, Union Never Lose" are being heard.

The union leader is leaving to see the boss. Negotiations are going to happen shortly.

Workers are asking for a forty-day bonus. A thirty day bonus is what the employer says. The hearts of the workers are praying that the negotiations should always succeed.

In the boss's chamber...

"Welcome chief...sit down..." soothing call from the boss in the A/C room further chills the union leader's body. He shyly sits on the expensive chair in front of him.

"Drinks....cool...or hot?..." the boss asked in a soft voice, "Coffee is enough sir..." says the leader.

After having coffee he slowly starts talking to the boss. "Last year you gave thirty-five days. All the workers are very dissatisfied now that suddenly five days have been reduced...."

The boss asks with a slight clearing of the throat. "Are you coming to the factory by walking...or by bus...?"

"I am coming by bus sir..."

"Dear Leader... it is a shame for me that you are coming in a bus...bike...scooter...atleast don't you want to come on a moped...okay I will arrange it..."

"As hearing that the factory in the neighborhood is giving more bonus, the workers are pressuring me a lot..."

"What TV do you have at home?"

"Color TV Sir"

"No No... how fast the country is progressing...go digital sir...ok ok...I will arrange"

The Leader is now sitting a little narrower in his chair. He speaks slowly.

"All the workers have started reading a lot...the workers in foreign countries are like this there...they are writing in the newspaper that they are like this...they are here also starting to talk after seeing this..."

"Hmm...Have you ever been on a foreign tour...?"

"No sir..."

"You will go to Singapore with family next month after saying to workers "I will go to the union conference". I will make arrangements..."

There is silence for a while. The leader gets up from the chair.

"Sir....then shall I leave...?"

"Mm... you started talking about some bonus...cut in the middle..." asks the boss looking at the Leader's face through his nose glass.

"Hmm...I'll manage sir..." After answering this, the Leader leaves the boss's room.

In the room where the workers have gathered, the slogans of "Workers' unity up up...The trade union has never lost..." are being heard.

******

5. GOT A JOB

Frustrated face. Unshaven head. File in hand. Name is Kumaran.

He entered a company on the main street. After giving copies of his school certificate, typing certificate etc. and fifty thousand rupees to the manager there, he looked at his face.

After checking everything he spoke. "Good bro. Anyway, you will be leaving for Kuwait in a month. You can expect our letter anytime."

He greeted him and came out.

At Egmore railway station he bought a ticket to Tambaram and boarded an electric train. He got a seat by the window. His memories raced back.

His mother said when he was going for the tenth government exam.

"Kumara....after your father's death, I have been living for you and your younger sister. After all these years of hard work, all the strength in my body has gone. The debilitating asthma also stuck with me. Our family will survive only if you get a job."

Kumaran wandered for work after passing tenth. "Give me one lakh. I will get you a job right away. A government official in the next street asked for a bribe.

"We can't trust anyone to give money..." Mom refused.

Kumaran appeared for railway jobs. Exam success. But he was called for an interview, he got failed.

Days, months and years flew by. Mother's condition remained the same.

"What about going abroad and earning?" The idea of a friend of Kumaran to give advice was very concerning to Kumaran.

He talked to his mother. Some expensive items from the house, jewelry were sold. Mom borrowed money from some places. Money added. Kumaran was coming after giving that money to the company. He had a kind of satisfaction.

The younger sister handed a letter to Kumaran as he entered the house. An interview order came from a life insurance company for the post of store clerk. He thought many times whether to go for the interview or not. Well, he decided to go ahead and went for the interview the next week. The officers asked him a lot of questions about the house.

"How long has it been since your father died?"

"What's Mom Doing"

"What is sister studying"

"Do you have any land of your own?"

After the interview it was boring to come home. However, it was a little comforting that the day to go to Kuwait was approaching.

A registered post arrived from the company in a few days. It also contained details of a ticket to Kuwait. Kumaran happily showed his mother and younger sister their faces withered.

"Brother...mother and I have never spent a single day without you...do you really want to go abroad..." asked her sister with tears in her eyes.

"Do you think this is the fate of people born in this country...I can't earn in my own land...don't cry..." Kumaran wiped his sister's tears. He consoled his mother.

Next week Kumaran went to Meenambakkam and took a flight. The mother and younger sister who had come to send them off stood watching the plane disappear in the sky.

When they got home, the girl next door brought a letter.

An order has arrived from the Life Insurance Corporation that asking Kumaran to join work the next day.

****

6. THE BEAUTY

After saying "we will go to our town and write letter" the people who had come to see Poongodi girl left. Tired of hearing the same answer over and over again, Poongodi sat down without any temptation. She knows that they politely told their dislike about her and left.

The old days flashed in Poonkodi's memory. She would have been ten years old then. With a tomato-like complexion and a lotus-like face, she is characterized by long black hair. Poongodi's mother combs each hair and applies oil to make it shiny. As her hair was reaching her ankles, even the teachers at school called her and asked her for advice on what to do to grow the hair.

Poonkodi, who was running like a deer and dancing like a peacock, was suddenly attacked by smallpox. She fought for her life and survived. But there are measles scars all over the face.

"Who lays eyes on my daughter, she becomes like this...the face of my beautiful doll changes with scars." Poonkodi's mother burst into tears.

After Poongodi's face change, she was not respected at school and in town. People who used to be friends with her and talked sweetly to her now started looking at her like a stranger. Poonkodi's heart began to warm with inferiority complex.

Her debut as a girl started when she was eighteen. Today she turns twenty-five years old. In the intervening seven years, many people have come and seen her, then written as 'not interested'. That punch of letters are kept in cupboard for a long time.

Poonkodi, who had shaken old memories, had now come to a conclusion. She told her parents. "I don't want to get married. I will get some job and stay with you."

About a week would have passed since she had made her decision. Dad came home in a hurry that day. "I have a guy who comes to see you evening. His name is Manimozhi. He works as a make-up artist in cine field. I met him through a friend. Get ready with well dressed...." But Poongodi refused.

"Dad...I have already said that I don't want to get married. I don't want to be humiliated again and again."

"Poongodi! This is guy of good character. Do just this once. If this is not right, I will not allow anyone to see you." Poongodi said "OK" because of her father's kind words.

Manimozhi came to see the girl with his mother, father and some friends. Poongodi emerged with coffee after everyone had had their snack. Everyone who took coffee looked up at her face and frowned. Only Manimozhi was sitting casually.

"We will tell you about one more week. What..." said Manimozhi's mother and looked at him. He said clearly. "Why it's been a long time. Tell it now. I have a crush on the girl. Ask her that does she has a like on me."

After that none of the people who came with Manimozhi spoke. Poonkodi was standing there in a state of pleasant surprise, unable to believe her ears.

The wedding ceremony took place in the very next month. Many celebrities from the film industry and media personalities came and congratulated him.

It was their first night. Poonkodi entered the bedroom and bowed to her husband's leg.

"Poongodi...I don't want all this respect. You and I are good friends and let's start our life okay...." He held her hands and made her sit on the bed.

she asked him, bowing her head. " I wish to know. Did you like me..."

"I told that on the day when I came to see the you..."

You are working in cinema. You have seen so many beautiful actresses..."

"Beauty..." he said and grinned. "Ask someone to explain what beauty is, no one can." He gently held her hands.

"You tell me to calm me down..."

"Poongodi....to know one thing. Everyone has a uniqueness in this world. I like your long hair very much."

"Don't you hate to see my ugly face?"

"I am the one who thinks that mental beauty is more important than facial beauty ..."

After that Poonkodi could not argue with him. Because he covered her lips with his lips.

****

7. EXPERIENCES

"I will have a felicitation ceremony at the Kamaraj Hall next Friday. The minister will also attend. You must come."

After telling Ganesan, Gopal got into the car and left.

Ganesan was looking at the direction the car had gone and the old programs about Gopal flashed in his mind

"How many interviews are there. Everything is pure eye-wipe. They have already selected the person and run the drama."

Ganesan remembered what Gopal had told him in frustration five years ago.

Ganesan and Gopal are graduates from the same college.

Ganesan got a job in his father's company when he retired. He married a woman of his relation and started to move his life in peace.

But Gopal got mire everywhere. Revile to him every day on behalf of his father, 'Eater without working'.

The job is not available. Did he win at least in love? No.

She fell in love with him and eventually went to London to marry the groom whom her parents had seen and settled down.

Gopal, who faced all these hardships, is a Great Person today. He is one of the most prolific writers in Tamil Nadu.

Kamarajar Arena was packed on the day of the ceremony. Ganesan got a seat as he arrived half an hour early.

One by one, the VIPs started arriving on stage. When the Minister and Gopal appeared on the stage, there was a cheer.

The ceremony has begun.

Everyone who spoke at the function showered praises on Gopal to such an extent that he shuddered and writhed.

After everyone's appreciation, Gopal came to the mic and started his thank you speech.

"You all praised me so much. Some said that my progress was due to hard work and some said that it was due to luck. Your reasons are correct. But I would like to humbly say that the most important reason for my growth is the fact that I have used the experiences I got to improve myself."

The crowd sat up in excitement.

Gopal continued.

"Though I attend many interviews I couldn't find the job. I couldn't marry the girl I fell in love with. I wrote two books with all these experiences. I titled "How to Succeed in Interview" and "How to Succeed in Love". These two books sold out several thousands. My life started to come up slowly. Apart from that, I have progressed by writing different kinds of books and standing before you today."

The audience including Ganesan applauded thoughtfully.

****

8. OPPORTUNITIES

"Today we are going to meet the famous Artist Kannan... who rose in life through his paintings...who is famous across the borders of Tamil Nadu and India...Hello Mr. Kannan..." The interview in T.V. started with the preface of the Interviewer.

"Hello everyone..." said Artist Kannan.

"Sir ... how many years have you painted ..."

"For about ten years ..."

"Would you please read out for the TV audience one or two of the remarkable letters of appreciation you have received...?"

Kannan handed some letters to the interviewer saying, "Oh...generous...".

First the interviewer read letters written by some fans from Tamil Nadu.

Next he read letters from different parts of India.

Next, when he read the letters that had come to him from abroad, lines of surprise crossed the interviewer's face.

The interview continued.

"In a very short period of time your name has spread all over the world...May you tell about what is the basic reason for your progress"

"The main reason is I used the opportunity correctly that I got."

"Can you explain a little...?"

"I was wandering as an unemployed youth then. But I had the ability to draw immediately whatever I saw... People of my house look at my drawing and say 'what ...If you scrawl like this, will you get food?.... They scolded saying, 'Look at the way to do some work'... But I don't know the way to get work... One day I was walking through Anna Flyover. Just side of the bridge is the US Embassy. There was some crowd at the door of that office. Now these days I find ten times of crowd like that I saw on those days.

"Yes sir...everyone has been waiting all day to get visa..."

"At that time, I didn't know about all this. Well... I started to have fun thinking that something was going on.

Everyone was excited. One of them was standing quietly leaning against the wall..."

"Who is he...?"

"He was not like our countryman. Also was not like a foreigner either. But he was standing quietly..."

"Then sir..."

"I liked his face very much. I started drawing him slowly on the paper I had..."

"Was in standing position...?"

"That's what I drew while leaning on the bridge wall..."

"All the vehicles had come and gone, sir..."

"Yes...I drew despite all that. It took about half an hour to finish the drawing..."

"Didn't he notice you at all...?"

"If he hadn't noticed, I think I would not have interview on television. He would have noticed that I was watching him... He came slowly towards me..."

"Then sir..."

"I was very scared...I was afraid that he was going to say something...but he came and bought the paper I had drawn...his face lit up...very good...he said 'very good' four times..."

There was a happiness on the face of the interviewer also.

Kannan continued.

"His name is Michael. He is a Tamil living in America. He works in a big art store there..He had come to visit a native in Tamil Nadu. He was standing there doing some work. Hmm...after praising me for a long time, he asked me for the paper I drew..."

"Did you give it, sir..."

"I gave it very happily. Only then he gave me the chance that change my life..."

"What sir is that...?" The interviewer asked with interest.

"He told me to prepare some good paintings and send them to his American address..."

"Oh... did you send it sir..."

"That's what I'm saying. I could have kept quiet thinking about why sending the painting to America... but I didn't miss the opportunity... I sent two or three paintings to him..."

Kannan was silent for a while. Then he said with a smile.

"The reception that started then for my paintings continues to this day... I owe him forever."

After talking about many more things the interviewer finally asked.

"Your advice to young people who want to advance in life sir..."

"Hopefully try...make sure to use the opportunity..."

"Thank you very much sir..." said the Interviewer.

"This is your picture.... I drew you while the interview was going on... "Artist Kannan gave him a piece of paper.

The Interviewer got up from his chair after seeing that.

"Wow.. Fantastic...thank you sir...thank you very much..." He shouted in surprise.

Then the picture was shown on television for the audience to see.

Everyone understood that Artist Kannan would not miss any opportunity.

****

9. WEALTHS

That night there was an argument between Kuppan and Saraswati for a few minutes.

"we give birth two children.... From now on we have to be careful, I say... but why don't you follow my words" Saraswati spoke a bit angrily.

"Hey...all this comes by itself...how do we see that careful or careless about this...?" Kuppan answered immediately.

Kuppan and Saraswati had been married for seven years. Two children, one boy and one girl, were born and the family has grown up.

Their location is the platform opposite the Rajiv Gandhi Government General Hospital, Chennai. Those who visit the Park Town area of Chennai know very well that many families have been living here for generations. This is near to Chennai MGR Railway Station. It is a surprising news that the people living here have ration cards and voting rights.

Kuppan and Saraswati are a couple born in two families here and married by their parents. Saraswati is a flower seller. Kuppan earns by driving a cart. Although their income was low, their life was going on happily.

But when his wife Saraswati is lying next to him at night, Kuppan becomes uncontrollable. Many times Saraswati tells him maturely, but he does not listen. That's why she was talking to him a bit angrily that day.

Hearing their loud talk, their six-year-old boy woke up from his sleep and said, "Saturns... I can't sleep...Be calm...Go to sleep..."

"He is like little leaf.... but.... look what he is talking about..." Kuppan said to Saraswati with concern.

"Yes..., he is your son...Isn't it? that's what he talks about..." Saraswati said a bit mockingly. After that there was less talk and a peaceful sleep began.

Saraswati woke up in the morning and woke up the children who were sleeping next to her. She patted Kuppan who was fast asleep and said "Inda....wake up..." and rolled up the kids's pillow covers.

She took the children to the public toilet make them bath and put them in a new dress. Kuppan was sitting up just then.

"Bai saw me on the way...he asked you to come to the shop at nine o'clock..." Kuppan hummed softly to Saraswati.

"This man has no other job...Take my breath in the early morning..."

"Aye....Almoner is calling and giving the work...you wrongly scold him..."

"Yes, he gives the big collector job! I should go with heavy load...pain in the back.... but, If I ask extra ten rupees he stares me as a stranger"

"Yes.... We can see money only with difficulty...Tell me if you want to make our kids study well...?".

"Hmm..... I'm pulling my cart hardly for these...Otherwise I'll be hammering the town with joy...".

While they were talking, the cell phone rang. The Bai called Kuppan.

"Hi...Did Saraswati say... Don't forget to come..."

"Told me, Bai...I'm leaving..." Kuppan got up quickly, "I'm coming after take a tea...prepare breakfast..."

He told Saraswati and left.

Saraswati lit the stove and dried the stone. She started pouring the dosa by mixing the wheat flour with spoon that had been thawed the night before.

"Maa... oftenly put this dosa...I don't understand at all..." The boy spoke in disgust.

"We will get some idli from shop for tomorrow ok..." she said and put the dosas on the plate for both of them. Both of them reluctantly started squeezing the dosa and stuffing it into their mouths. Saraswati gave Kuppan two dosas on a plate as he returned after drinking tea. He looked up at her like a model and started eating without saying anything.

Saraswti take the children to school and Kuppan left with cart for Bai shop. After leaving the children at school, Saraswati went to the Koyambedu market and bought flowers. When returned to residence she decided to sleep for a while and spread out the mat.

But the sound of a lorry on the road woke her up within minutes. Wiping her face with a saree scarf, she took a string and started tying it with flowers. While she was blooming fast for a while Sumathi who lives next door, came with saying "Sister..." and sat near her. She took and arranged flowers, then gave to Saraswati.

"What is Sumathi...your face is a kind of wither...?

She said "Nothing Sister..."

"No, you are lying...Anyway, tell me, Sumathi...'

Sumathi was quiet for a few seconds and then started talking slowly.

"They are trying to tie him up with other girl..."

Sumathi was dating a boy who lived in the next street. He belongs to a wealthy family. On the day before he had told Sumathi that his family is seeing a girl elsewhere. That is what Sumathi anxiously told Saraswati.

Saraswati got angry.

"Didn't I tell you one day...that these rich people how use poors like us and get away ...you didn't listen..."

'No... he is strong...he says that we can run away and get married... "

"Oh...If you do well, I will be happy..."

Sumathi's mother suddenly spoke up.

"Hi...what are you doing there...Didn't I tell you to dry all these clothes..."

"Sister...I'm leaving...I'll back later..."Saraswati watched Sumathi without blinking who was going.

She remembered the brutality that had happened to Kala who studied with Saraswati in school seven or eight years ago. She fell madly in love with the compounder who worked at the hospital. There is no place in Chennai where the two of them don't hang out together. Finally, his family forced him to marry another girl and Kala commited suicide by jumping in front of an electric train. She is saddened to think that Sumathi is in a similar predicament.

Her daughter's class teacher smiled and spoke to Saraswati as she went to school collect children in afternoon. "Hey...do you know how your girl is dancing...Does she learn dance somewhere?"

"That's nothing, teacher.... For learning these all where is money with us? She just watch TV and dance...that's all..."

"No... if you train her, she will become a great person in the future..."

Saraswati was proud. "Okay...I'm leaving teacher..." she said and left with the children.

"Today menu is sambar rice in school ... super taste mom..."Saraswati's boy exclaimed and also said that his younger sister was not eating properly.

"Don't eat?..." Saraswati asked, "Maa...Terribly alkaline" She said in a childish voice.

"Okay come on...I'll buy some chocolate and go..." she said and picked her up and kept in hip.

Kuppan came at three in the evening and asked Saraswati. "Hi....Did you have meals...?"

"That's the old rice left in vessel... I touched the pickle and emptied it..." She asked, "Did you eat...?"

"Why do you ask that drama... I was standing there unloading the parcels of the Bai shop... Suddenly call from Owner Lal. He wanted me to go to Rayapettah with luggage...I went to that place and made the delivery. When I sat with fatigue...my stomach rumbled...I saw the biryani shop on the side...the smell lifted my breath...I went in without speculation..." Saraswati interrupted to tell Kuppan.

"What are you...you are king"

"Don't be sarcastic, hear me...the people in the neighborhood were bitten...The supplier came and asked me "Mutton or Chicken?... I asked what the rate was?...he said the Mutton was twice the price of the Chicken...here is some virus...that's why everyone is eating Mutton . I thought about it...we want to have a full stomach...I decided that's what we need...I had chicken biryani...I closed my eyes and emptied the plate"

"Are you saying it's a virus...you come and sing..." Saraswati asked worriedly.

He took the money from his pocket and gave it to Saraswati as he said philosophically, "Adipodi...death will come anytime...whether it is by virus or vomiting."

"I will lie down and wake up within one hour...you all three get ready...let's go to Natraj theater..."

"What!..We watched the movie last week...Is it the next movie...?"

"Keep quiet...Tala picture has been running...It is great...My friend said...Start silently without saying anything..."

"If you told me in the morning, I wouldn't have come to buy flowers..."

"Give it to Meenakshi and she will sell that"

Parvathiyammal, a neighbor, saw her tying her sari and combing the children's hair with powder.

"What Saraswati...where do you go..."

" To Natraj Theater to watch a movie..."

"Ha...You are lucky.... Your man worked like a bullock...So You can watch as many films as you want...".

Saraswati replied angrily.

"Parvati Sister... You don't keep eye...six months ago you spoke something like this...He was lying in ill for a week...still talking the same way..."

"I'm sorry... I just asked for something.. You are talking about something... Now on I won't say anything...." Parvati moved away.

They left to watch movie. To go to the theatre, you have to cross the road and walk that way.

"I will come after drinking a tea.... stand there..."Kuppan went to the side bunk shop.

Saraswati muttered "You do one by one when we go..." She took the children and stood on the side of the road.

As it was a busy road, the vehicles were coming and going fast. As the red signal fell, all vehicles were forced to stop.

An expensive car pulled up in front of where Saraswati and the children were standing. A red-faced woman was sitting inside the shiny car. Seeing the shine of the car, both the children started touching the car with their hands.

After drinking tea, Kuppan arrived and shouted at the children.

"Hey.... Don't touch the car.... the people inside are going to fight..." he said looking at the boy and pulling his daughter. Saraswati said to Kuppan in surprise.

"Look how shiny the car is...I have never seen a car like this..."

"May it be foreign car!..." Kuppan said.

"Yes... how many blessings the people inside have got, for come in this car..."

"You say correct..."Kuppan replied and warned. "Mm... The signal may change... Let's cross speedily"

Kuppan picked up his daughter. Saraswati held her son's hand and started walking fast across the road.

The woman sitting inside the car was watching them go through the window. A kind of longing sigh emerged from her who was childless even after ten years of marriage.

****

10. LOVE

While she boarded the plane in New York, the excitement and joy that had not been there infected Gauri in Chennai.

It was an indescribable joy to step off the plane and set foot on the ground. Does everyone feel this way when it comes to motherland?

When Gauri came out with mom, dad and younger brother Shekhar's family after the routine checks, her elder brother Shankar was waiting with the car.

"Hi Uncle..."

Shekhar's children cheered towards Shankar.

"What... Was the journey comfortable...?"

Shankar asked his father.

"No problem. Only your Mom met some trouble"

"What...what do you...?" Shankar asked Mom.

"Nothing. I'm just getting old. I got ache little bit on my head and vomit. That's all."

"Gauri how are you."

"I'm All Right"

Then he looked at younger brother's family and gave a fake smile.

"Hmm...let's go"

Everyone nods to his question and the car starts. Shankar drove the car.

Gauri's memories run flash back fifteen years.

How furious Shankar spoke that day.

"Dad...are you wondering if Gauri only goes to the office...do you know if she also goes to the park and the beach?"

"Gauri...what does brother say"

Dad asked softly.

Gauri got angry with Shankar.

"Yes. What my brother says is true. I like a guy named Gunaseelan. I went to the beach with him one day. I think brother saw that."

Her mom and dad were a bit shocked to hear this.

"Oh...love..."

Shankar looked at Gauri scornfully.

"Dad....she has gone to work. There is no fate that we have to eat by her earning. Tell her to leave the office. Find a good place and get married right away."

"Why...I told you that I like someone. You tell me to look elsewhere."

"Don't speak ignorantly...what is our caste, what is his caste...um...let go of caste. status..Can the ladder reach us and him? Hmm...you don't have to go to work from tomorrow...do you understand..."

"Brother...I really love him. Without him I have no life..."

Shankar stared at Gauri for a while and said.

"If that's your decision, then ask my decision too. If you marry him, don't see my face after that."

He spoke angrily and turned to his mother.

"Mom.. If you and father agree to this, I will go home alone with my wife and child."

When Shankar said that he was leaving the hereditary home, his mother was upset. She asked Gauri frantically.

"Why all this..."

Shankar spoke to father in an authoritative tone.

"Dad...what if you didn't speak and remained silent? What was your decision?"

"Shankar...what should I do...Gauri is the only girl in our house. Can I make her suffer?"

"Mm... Maa... have you thought about what your brother is saying...?" He asked Gauri.

"Dad....caste, status with this world has been suppressing love since that time. I have one decision. If I get married, it will be with him."

"Then I will go alone tomorrow."

Shankar finally got up.

"Separate stay...why do you hurt my heart to talk like this" mother cried.

The next day, mother's fever worsened and she was admitted to the hospital.

"You all have to cooperate so that she can have peace of mind..." advised the doctor.

"Brother...think of mother. Does't happen anything wrong to mother..." Gauri glared at Shankar.

"Then listen to me. Forget him."

There was a phone call from America when mom was getting better. Shekhar invited Mom, Dad and Gauri to come to America.

"If I go to America..."Gauri thought with her mind turned to stone.

That day she went to America with her mother and father, where she spent fifteen years as a typist in a company. She has also acquired American citizenship.

In between, whenever mom and dad came back to Chennai, she stayed in America.

Shankar's daughter had come of mature age only a month ago. Shankar had sent a mail saying that he must bring Gauri for the ceremony of his daughter. Gauri saw Shankar's daughter as a child. The affection felt when he knew that she had grown up prompted him to visit her.

That is why Gauri had come to Chennai after all these years.

The car was passing Saidapet when Gauri lost her thoughts.

Mother asked touching her with her hand.

"Gauri...what are you thinking..."

"Nothing..."

"Madras has changed a lot..."

"Mm... did you tell me that the name has changed to Chennai..."

Mom smiled hearing Gauri speaking politely.

When the car arrived home, the sister-in-law greeted them with a smile.

Gauri woke up in the afternoon after eating tiffin in the morning.

He heard others talking outside the room.

"Gauri remains unchanged.. Girl, don't she want to get married and have a family" - this is Sister-in-law.

"What do we do? Shankar told her not to marry the boy she liked. She wad stubborn and told no for marriage..." Mother spoke sadly.

Shankar said.

"I don't think she will be stubborn just like this. Otherwise, I will not stand in the way of her's love."

"You could force someone to tie the knot in America."-This is sister-in-law.

"She won't eat for two days if we talk about her wedding. All she always remembers Gunaseelan who got used to her"

Shekhar's wife said softly.

"Gauri is now forty years old. Somehow you all have ruined her life. If Gauri had got married, by now the two beauties would have been playing with each other..."

Gauri sat up slowly with old memories.

How will Gunaseelan look now? How many children will he have? Will he be angry when see me?

In Gauri's mind there was a desire to see Gunaseelan.

The next day she left without telling anyone. A couple of people who saw her on the street where Gunaseelan's house was, said, "It looks like I have seen someone...somewhere".

"Will he stay in the same house. Or has he moved house?" Thinking that when Gauri reached home a boy was playing at the door with Gunaseelan's comparison. She called him and inquired.

"Mr. Gunaseelan is there..."

"Wait a minute"

The boy went inside. In the next minute, Gunaseelan emerged. No change in appearance. Silver hairs only on the head.

"Does he recognize me?"

Contrary to Gauri's thoughts, Gunaseelan welcomes him.

"Come Gauri...come in..."

He took her to the first room inside the house and asked her to sit on a chair Gunaseelan sat leaning on the opposite chair and stared at her for a few seconds. Then he put a finger on his forehead and closed his eyes and thought. There was silence for two minutes.

"What to eat..."

He asked Gauri softly opening his eyes.

"No... don't want anything."

"Hmm how are you?

"I am the same..."

"Your husband and children...?"

"That's what I said...I am the same as I was here"

"I don't understand what you mean..."

"I went to America without telling you. But I can't leave your memory alone...then how can I get married? Let it go.. You don't introduce your wife and children to me...I saw that it was your son..."

"He is son of my younger brother."

"Oh...your wife and children...?"

"Only when marriage is happened, about having a wife and children"

"What do you say"

"How can I marry another woman after you are so deep in my heart?"

Neither of them could speak after that. They sat looking at each other in silence. Both their eyes were fillng of tears. Time was running on.

****

11. SAVOURS

"Girl without little bit of savour..."

Vasanth mumbled while eating. His wife Vasuki, who was heading towards the kitchen, looked back and asked.

"What do you...want?"

"Mm... want the savour..." Vasanth said slowly.

"What do you mean..." she stared him with confusion.

"Nothing...I told you it's time for office..." he changed his words.

"Eat slowly...there is time..." She said with a smile and entered the kitchen.

Vasanth works in a government office.

He got married only a month ago. His wife Vasuki is his close relation. She grew up in the village.

Vasanth studied and grew up in Chennai. Due to his mother's insistence, he reluctantly agreed to the marriage. But Vasuki's tastes were different from Vasanth's.

After finishing his meal, Vasanth told his mother and left quickly.

His mother came to him and said softly.

"Hey...do tell Vasuki...bring flowers for her in evening..."

"Ah...that's the only downside."

He ignored his mother's speech and left.

He and Mala sit side by side in the office and work together. All eyes fall on them.

" Vasanth is very lucky. He is blessed to be near to Mala all time..."

"He has good mole in his body...Otherwise, does he get a chance like this...?"

"Just like husband and wife they smile...they eat the same...they leave together..."

So many reviews about them. That day during the meal Mala asked Vasanth.

"What's up Vasanth...how is your new wife...do you like her...Does she like you ?..."

"Destiny," replied Vasanth in one word.

"Why... what happened...?"

Mala asked a bit shocked.

"Nothing...my taste and her taste are different..."

"You said she is educated girl..."

"What did she study..."

Vasanth was bored.

"Then Vasanth...Yesterday I read an English novel. It was written by a female author. Do you know how it was...?"

"Mm... you know...but she...one day I asked if she had read any novel...?

"In our house, we don't have enough time to cook..."she simply replied.

"I think she is cooking expert."

"Do you know what was the last movie you watched before marriage..."

"What movie..."

"Complete Ramayana..."

Mala said after smiling for a while.

"Poor village girl..."

"I told you this is fate. Do you understand...?" He said in frustration.

At this time Udayan came there saying "Hello Vasanth...Hello Mala...".

"Come on...what a long time to see you"

Vasanth called Udayan and made him sit next to him.

"I went to home town for an important job...that's a week leave..."

"So... can you eat..."

"I am just eating. Then...how is married life...what does your wife say...?"

Udayan patted Vasanth's back.

Vasanth looked at Mala without saying anything. Mala said sarcastically.

"Udayan...Vasanth is very emotional...His wife is pure folk."

"Is that so..."Udayan casually asked,

"Okay...we'll see then" he said and left.

When Vasanth went home that day, he felt ache in head. Even taking pills did not help.

"Can we go to the doctor...?" asked Vasanth's mother.

"Hm..." he nodded.

"Don't do that. I will give 'Kasaya'..." said Vasuki and she prepared it within half an hour.

"I just don't want to smell it. I'm sorry..."

Vasanth reluctantly bought it and drank it. He fell asleep within five minutes.

Vasanth was sleeping on the bed. Mala came near him. She gently put her hand on his forehead.

He woke up.

"Mala...are you..." she asked him "does your head hurt..." in a soft voice.

He gently held her hand and made her sit on the bed. Mala bent down and put her lips on his lips.

Vasanth woke up startled by the sound of "Hmm...wake up...it's gone...". Vasuki was standing opposite.

A wistful sigh escaped him as he realized what had happened was a dream. Vasanth was surprised to sit up.

The headache had gone somewhere. Everything is the work of "Kasaya". He showered and ate with enthusiasm and left for office.

Vasanth's mother complimented Vasuki, "Dear...you did get rid of the headache!"

Vasanth was thinking about the dream that he had yesterday night at the office. That day Mala came in a new saree. The shine of the saree caught everyone's eyes.

Vasanth said hesitantly to her while eating.

"Mala...the saree is so beautiful..."

"Only the saree...?"

Mala questioned.

"It's you too..." he choked out the words and looked at her closely.

"I want to say something.The word just won't come."

"Anything can be known only by telling..."

Mala spoke without giving up.

Suddenly Mala's friend came there and the conversation stopped.

When Vasanth went home that day, he sat down and thought.

"Mala... if I get..."

Sweet to think. He took out a pop music cassette and played it in the tape recorder. He was enjoying it by swinging his legs to the music.

Vasuki, who had brought coffee, frowned after hearing the sound of the song. "What is this song... I don't understand anything..."

Vasanth suddenly stopped the song and said sternly.

"Hm... this is a song for intellectuals..."

"Isn't it...sing the village like this...but you will understand well..."She sang a folk song with raga.

As she sang, Vasanth stared at her in amazement. It surprised him that a pop song and a folk song were almost at the same tune.

The next day when Vasanth told Mala and Udayan about this in the office, "Really..." Both of them were surprised.

Next week, Udayan came to Vasanth's house on an errand.

Seeing him on the way, Vasanth took him home. He asked him to have lunch. Udayan started eating "I have never eaten this delicious in my life..." Saying that, Vasuki's face turned red with embarrassment.

After the meal, Vasanth and Udayan were sitting alone and talking.

Udayan asked, "Did you see how your wife's face turned red when I told you that the food was delicious? Have you even praised her like this?"

Vasanth thought and said "No".

"You don't know how to appreciate the talent of a wife...you don't understand the taste of that woman...you say that she is a person who has no taste in this way of mind..."

"My taste is different..."

"Anyway how everyone has the same taste...everyone in the world has different talents...There is a different taste... Life will be delicious only if you understand this and adjust it. Do you follow me?..."

After a moment of silence, Vasanth slowly intervened.

Next day he came to office thinking about many things.

That day Mala was much smiling and talking to everyone. Vasanth didn't know what was the reason for her happiness.

After some time she said softly to Vasanth.

"Vasanth there is a turning point in my life..."

"What...?"

Vasanth asked expectantly.

"I will go to London next week...My uncle's family is there. I will stay there..."

Vasanth looked at her shocked. He asked after thinking for a few seconds.

"Are you going to resign from your job...?"

"Yes...I can get a better job in London.. Uncle has sent a letter saying that the salary is also high..."

"Staying here and going there for so long... do you like that situation..."

"What's the point...you just have to change your taste...you just have to adjust..."

Vasanth was unable to speak after that. After office she said, "Bye...Bye..." Vasanth's heart was heavy when she left from there. He slowly start to leave for home. On the way, he thought about the events after the wedding one by one.

His mental confusion seemed to be resolved. Vasuki's face came before his mind's eye.

****

12. THE FORTUNE

Everyone was unhappy for a month in Muthuswamy's house, who works at the post office. His wife does not talk to him properly. His two daughters were just answering the questions like third persons.

Even the mother-in-law who came from time to time was visibly angry. Only the five-year-old son was crawling affectionately "Daddy...Daddy..." If he also knew the details, would he have behaved like them?

The reason for all this was a rat that came into the house a month ago. On that day Muthusamy was watching T.V. at night time. Suddenly the rat jumped on his leg and ran quickly into the kitchen. No matter how hard everyone searched that night, it never came out.

Muthusamy, who had left early the next morning for a job, said to his wife, "Somehow find the rat and drive it away. It will bite and destroy all the clothes." He left after saying that.

When he returned home in the evening, a happy news awaited him. His eldest daughter had an interview from Bank. He was very happy when his daughter came and told him this.

After some time, after having coffee, he asked his wife about the rat.

She said, "Put all the utensils aside. What you said is wrong. It's not a rat. It's a little mouse. (Vehihle of God Ganesh) It entered the room and went under the cot. There's a lot of bundles under the cot. I left it so we can look at it tomorrow.

That night, his five-year-old son woke up screaming as mouse jumped on him. The next day Muthuswamy took him to the doctor because he had a fever.

"It's nothing. It's just a normal fever," the doctor treated him with an injection.

When he returned home from office that evening, his wife brought a letter. It was written by his brother-in-law. He said in the letter that he had got a job in the railways and had sent a thousand rupees through money order to show his happiness.

"I think the money order will come tomorrow." said the wife.

The "expendable" he said and asked, "How is the child's body? That rat is gone."

"No. I have a bit of work to do today. So I can't put all the stuff away. Hmm...and another thing. Grandma of next door said that it is luck when a mouse come to house. Look, our girl got an interview from Bank. My brother has got a job," said the wife hesitantly.

"You don't know that I don't like this kind of faith. Yesterday it climbed on the child and ran. He was lying down with a fever. What if you bother me again..."

"I don't think the rat would have climbed on him. He must have had a bad dream. That's why he screamed."

"You imagine and say something. Hmm...for tomorrow just push it away...okay..."

She was silent for a while and then said, "Mm."

But the next day she did not try to chase away the rat.

Muthuswamy, who went to the office that day, was in for a pleasant surprise.

An order came from Delhi as to pay the bonus balance to the employees, which had been dragging on for months.

He returned home in the evening and told his wife this happy news. She said, " All this because of the fortune that the rat came to our house. How long have you been talking about this matter. Now the money has arrived."

He asked angrily "Another Rat Myth.. Did you drive it away today...or not...?"

"No..."

"You don't care if the boy gets a fever...it doesn't matter if the rice dal clothes are empty...it's the sentiment that matters..."

"No... what did I come to say..." she trailed off. Hearing the loud talk of the two, the three children came there.

"Okay, well...you won't do as I say...tomorrow is Sunday. I'll see and chase that rat away myself...um...go, go...look at work..."

Muthusamy shouted and everyone dispersed

The next day after his strenuous efforts the rat left the house. When it went out, Muthuswamy's wife gave a longing sigh.

From the next day, problems started coming to them one by one. He took four days off to see Muthuswamy's mother when he received a letter from the town saying that she was seriously ill. It cost about two thousand rupees.

"Drive away the rat that came to do good for our family. Look now. Unexpected expenses have come"

His wife told him gently.

"No one in the world is going to get sick. It's not going to cost. It's going to be a knot for anything."

Muthusamy said angrily.

The following week the daughter went to the bank interview looking sad.

She inquired, "I failed in interview dad...".

Muthuswamy was sad.

"You won't believe what I said...if that creature was in our house, would she have failed like this...?"

His wife increased his grief.

"Mm... you start...seeing what you're talking about, it's as if you're saying that the reason for everything is that rat. cha...cha..."

She hurriedly went into the kitchen to talk to him with disgust.

The little girl's neck chain went missing, the newly bought T.V. got repair which cost two hundred rupees, the boy not getting a seat in a higher school Muthuswamy's wife linked everything to the rat.

The idea that he chased away the rat was the cause of all the problems in the house, and everyone except Muthusamy began to feel a little bit. Everyone started seeing him as a criminal.

This is the unhappy situation in his family for a month.

There was no train for half an hour due to power cut that day. The officer angrily asked Muthusamy as he was late to the office.

"Why are you coming so late? Have you thought office as your home..."

Muthuswamy, who was already in trouble, got furious.

"Why sir...the house is so bad...we come to work for the house" he answered briefly.

The officer then went silent. Within a few days he showed his authority and transferred Muthusamy to a faraway post office.

Now going to office has become a big problem for him. He have to leave home at seven o'clock in the morning. He can reach home only at eight o'clock in the night. He succumbed to typhoid fever due to excessive wandering.

Due to his wife's constant care, he returned to his old health within a month. But loss of salary for a fortnight. Even as he lay feverish, she kept telling him about the mouse.

He started going to office after vacation. But the body was weak.

All the friends advised him, "Why are you doing dull? Take care of your body."

As he was returning home on the train, he remembered the events of the past month.

"Perhaps whether it may be good that the rat was not chased away?"

He asked himself.

Early the next morning, his wife woke him up from his bed.

"Nothing. Someone has come looking for you. He says there is an important matter. He wants to see right now."

Muthusamy got up and came out.

The lottery ticket dealer was standing.

"Good morning Sir... the lottery ticket you bought last night won five lakh rupees sir"

He said with full of teeth in mouth.

A wave of happiness flowed through Muthuswamy's mind. Though he asked with doubt.

"How did you know that the prize fell on my ticket"

"The fact is Sir...the one you bought was the last ticket sold in our shop. That's what I could find correctly...look here...there is number on the Newspaper..."

The dealer handed over the paper. Muthusamy went inside the house and quickly brought the lottery ticket. He checked the number on the paper and gave it back excitedly.

"Very happy...do you have coffee..."

"None of that sir. If you come to deposit the ticket in the bank, I will also stand and take a photo. I even called the press office and told them."

"Hmm...I'll be back in Bank in an hour. OK..."

"Thank you very much sir. I will come then."

When he left, the house was filled with chaos. Everyone sat around Muthuswamy and started talking.

"Alright. Leave quickly. Journalists are going to wait at the bank."

The wife said, nervous and happy.

Muthuswamy was about to take a bath and eat and was ready to leave when she came near.

She said, "May luck always be on your side. I hurt your feelings by saying words without knowing something. Forgive me..." and Muthusamy looked up her.

Her gaze rested on the lottery ticket in his hand.

"Okay okay...let it be what happened..." he said and left.

When he left the house, a rat was entering the house without anyone's knowledge.

****

13. THE NATURE

When the express train stopped at Salem Junction, Dinakar got out of the first-class coach.

Two people standing on the platform with garlands questioned him with flushed faces.

"Engineer Mr. Dinakar..."

"Yes.. I am."

When Dinakar said that, they put the small garlands they had in their hands on his neck.

"Welcome sir. We have been appointed as two assistants for you. We have brought a jeep for you sir" They took the suitcase from him.

"Oh...thank you" Dinakar took off the garlands and gave them to them.

He adjusted his clothes and started walking with them.

When they came out of the station, the wind was blowing pleasantly.

He and his assistants boarded the jeep parked there and the jeep took off on the road marked Rasipuram.

Dinakar asked, "Are all ready to stay?"

"All the arrangements are ready sir. Even the phone connection has been got..."

"Very good.. Demolition is due to start in two weeks...will there be enough people for the job?"

"We have prepared everything from neighbouring villages sir..."

"Why did those villagers go to where?"

"Mm... a little trouble sir..." Dinakar asked hurriedly as the assistant hesitated. "What trouble...any problem...?"

"Nothing Sir...a boy named Tamilarasan...he had gathered all the people of that village and held a demonstration that the trees and plants in this place should not be destroyed..."

"Bastard..."

Dinakar cursed in his heart.

His memories flashed back.

Dinakar's family is a middle-class. After his father died at a young age, his mother made him study with her hard efforts.

After he completed his engineering, he got his two younger sisters married with the money he got from small contracts.

He married a girl who liked him when he was in college with his mother's consent.

His life was moving as a family with a five-year-old boy and a three-year-old girl.

But his financial dream of making big money was not fulfilled. It was at this time that a great opportunity came to him.

A Japanese company got a contract to complete the construction of a new raw film factory in Tamilnadu.

Once this work is completed, many lakhs will come to him. The factory was to be built after clearing a forest area in Kollihills upland. Dinakar had come now to complete the work of clearing the forest area in the first phase.

He asked his assistants as he recovered from his old memories. "Hm... what is that Youth's name?"

"Sir Tamilarasan..."

"Why don't build a factory...Environment protection...Does he say something like this..."

"Sir, he says that he is going to do some herbal research in this forest area..."

"Be a herbalist...be a researcher...be a mad man. Are you telling that such a big factory should not be built for that?

"Little boy...we think he will consent if we say it on appropriate way."

"Ok ok...make sure nothing comes in the way of our work"

"Ok sir"

The jeep was going beyond Rasipuram. The beauty of Kolli hills started to show little by little.

It was getting dark when they reached Belukurichi.

After stopping the jeep at a place, one of the Assistants got down and said, "Sir...I have bought food." In a few minutes the jeep took off again with the huge carrier.

"This is the road to Goovaimalai Murugan Temple" they introduced to Dinakar. After a few kilometres, a specially constructed office building was seen on the side of the road. It was small but elegant.

After getting down from the jeep and going inside, they opened a room saying "this is your room sir".

Dinakar liked the layout of the room. Dinner ended satisfactorily.

"Where are you going to lie down?" Dinakar asked the attendants.

"There is a place in the back, sir. Let's put a bench and sleep... Good night, sir..." They both went outside and Dinakar went to sleep.

He was excited when he woke up in the morning. He opened the window and looked. The beauty of the mountain and the greenery of the trees and plants were breathtaking. He was wiping his face after taking a bath.

Suddenly there was a noise outside. Words that didn't sound right at first became clear after a while.

"Don't destroy don't destroy...don't destroy forests..."

"Don't spoil don't spoil...don't spoil people's lives..."

"Let's save...let's save the natural wealth..."

Dinakar opened the door and came out.

About a hundred people had come towards his place.

They did not stop chanting even after reaching the place where Dinakar was standing.

Seeing the crowd, he got a little scared. However, he mustered up the courage.

"Mm... stop...who are you...what do you all want..." he asked loudly.

"We are the people of this village You must not destroy this forest area. This is our demand..." The young man at the front of the crowd spoke.

"Who are you...what's your name?" Dinakar asked angrily.

"Tamilarasan sir..."

Dinakar remembered what the assistants had told him when he arrived.

"Why not destroy the forest. Environmentally safe...?"

"That is one reason sir...but there is another important reason. There are some wonderful herbs in this forest area. They have said in the Siddhar books. If forest get destroyed all the herbs will also be destroyed."

"Which century are you in? If someone ever wrote and hid it, do you trust it and make such a mess..."

"No one sir...the wise Siddhars of our country have written this"

"Do you know anything about Siddha medicine? Who are the Siddhars? When did they exist? Do you have any evidence for this?"

"I have taken a diploma in Siddha medicine sir...but I have not finished reading about the Siddhars yet...the ideas of the Siddhars have come in a book now. Their knowledge is like a deep sea...it will take a long time to know it all, sir..."

"Have you come to fight without fully knowing a thing?"

"Are there rare herbal plants in this area that can cure all incurable diseases? Siddhars have written a note...Our grandfather also said a lot about this. He is also a Herbal doctor..."

"Mr... Everyone is going to London and America to study medicine, came back and practice. Do you know how much medical science has developed...you have been talking about some herb and this..."

"Our country's medicine is natural medicine sir. This is the only glory. The cost is also less expensive sir. But our forefathers did not write in detail about this. That's why we can't take this to the people quickly. No matter how much you try other medical methods, some diseases can only be partially controlled. But we can heal completely with our Siddha medicine."

Dinakar was irritated by Tamilarasan's unrelenting retorts. He understood that he would not get his way.

"Come on matter man...now what to do"

"Sir. I have researched the herbs of this area. I will prepare good medicines as soon as possible. Sir...in this situation please don't destroy the forest..."

Dinakar made some calculations in his mind. After thinking for a while he said.

"You all go. I will call Chennai and talk to the superiors about your request. I will let you know in two days...Ok..."

"Thank you very much sir" said Tamilarasan with a smile on his face and there was lively noise arise among the crowd.

"Then we leave sir"

When he left, the crowd followed him. Dinakar's body was hot with anger as he watched them go. As assistants heard that, they came running in a frenzy. "Sir...what happen?"

"Nothing. That Tamilarasan group came to meet me and demanding..."

"Did they threaten something sir..."

"No no. He's a good guy. But when he is with crowd something view unusual..."

"May we ask for police protection, sir?"

"Hmm...don't go to that extent. We have to deal with this matter in a different way...Ok...if you do that..."

"Tell us sir..."

"Get that boy here alone tomorrow...I'll talk..."

They met Tamilarasan at his home the next day and told him that Dinakar wanted to see him alone. He also came unannounced.

Dinakar asked Tamilarasan to sit on the chair in front of him.

"Brother, have tea..." he said.

"Thanks sir...I just came after eat" Tamilarasan politely refused.

"Then....I called Chennai yesterday and spoke to the officials. They are very sympathetic. They made hard efforts buying this factory order... They fear all may be wasted by your demands." Dinakar told Tamilrasan a series of lies.

"Sir...I have been doing herbal research in this area for a year. I am persuading so far because this research is beneficial to people..." Tamilarasan spoke clearly.

"Brother...you must understand what I am saying...this is no ordinary project...They are investing crores of rupees...if this stops, it will be a huge loss for them."

"They can move a little further and start that, sir..."

"Why don't you go somewhere else and do some research?"

"It is in this area that I hope to find the original herbs I mentioned..Siddhar note also says the same sir..."

Dinakar suddenly got angry. "Herb...Herb...what is this...everyone has left a rocket for the moon and Mars. What are you, you are a pure ignorant..."

"Of course not sir. I have done this research with full thought. If my research is successful, it will benefit the human race..."

"Do you want to do anything practical? Tell me if you write honey on paper and it will be sweet. That's right...where did you study?"

"Sir in Belukurichi till SSLC.. I completed my degree in Salem. Siddha medicine course in Chennai sir..."

"Study in Chennai!" Dinakar asked in surprise.

"Yes sir..."

"Hey... did you study in Chennai? Even you don't understand the world. Have you seen there...everyone makes a plan and moves forward..."

"Yes sir...the people there don't care about anything...money is their goal..."

"What's wrong with that. Money is everything..You don't get it right. That's why you have done all this research and wasted your diet..."

"Sir, only if the body is healthy, there will be peace in life..."

"Isn't that all behind... first is money. Do you know what my goal is? Save as much money as you can and have fun and enjoy life with your friends. Ok ok...you don't understand all this now. Listen to me. Get a job soon. Get married immediately and settle down in life. Ok...um...I will arrange an amount for you. O.K..."

"Please sir. I don't want anything. I don't have any other thoughts... I want to succeed in herbal research. That is my goal. I am asking you to fall at your feet. Please don't destroy the forest..."

Tamilarasan's eyes began to water.

"Che...che...Why do you go cry over all this...you go home. Everything will be fine."

Tamilarasan got up half-heartedly to tell Dinakar and left.

When he was gone Dinakar closed his eyes and began to think. After a while he asked the attendants.

"Who is he? Is he so stubborn?"

The assistant gave details about Tamil Rasan.

"He is a lonely man sir... his mother died when he was a child. His family has been making folk remedies for generations. His grandfather's name is Guruswamy Poet. Father's name is Saminathan Poet. After his grandfather, his father left medicine and started farming...he died two years ago. After that he got involved in inheritance business. After completing his studies in psychiatry, he have done medicine and research.

The news in the next day's paper shocked Dinakaran.

The news about Tamilarasan's protest was published in a small way under the title "Demonstration in Belukurichi".

"Rascal...seems to have messed up our plans..."

Dinakar said slowly in his mind. He started thinking about what to do before the matter escalated. One of his Assistants asked Dinakar hesitantly. "Sir...may we put him to death..."

"No. Your idea is wrong. There are people behind him...if we do this will be turbulent. Mater will go big. It is danger to us..."

"Another way sir..."

"The only way is to separate the crowd behind him from him." Dinakar spoke while rubbing his cheek with his hand.

"Good idea sir..." the Assistant complimented his plan.

Within the next week, their plan was perfectly executed. People were separated from Tamilarasan using all the weapons of politics, money and caste.

"We will be victorious only if we all fight together..." The words of Tamilarasan did not appeal to the people.

"Brother. Your idea is good. But we also have a family. We also have to behave...excuse us..."

He stood as a lone tree so that everyone could stand aside.

For the next few days he suffered from sleeplessness. Not eating properly. Almost like a psycho.

That day he received a message that the tree fellers were coming. He quickly ran to the road. He stood in the middle of the road and stopped the big lorries that were coming loaded with machines.

"I won't let this machine go...I won't allow destroy the forest."

Tamilarasan stand with arms spread out.... The driver got down and squirrelled with him for the way..... A small crowd had gathered.

By then Dinakar got the news and came quickly with his helpers in a jeep.

"Hi man...why are you crazy...do you go to order or not...do I call the police..." Dinakar shouted.

"Don't destroy the forest...don't destroy the forest..." Tamilarasan was saying again and again.

"Why are you watching...are you going to meet him...or have I filed a police complaint..."Dinakar looked at the group and asked.

There was a small commotion in the crowd.

Two people came and grabbed Tamilarasan and tried to drag him away. He refused to move using all his strength. Two more people came and four of them took him away.

"Don't destroy the forest...don't destroy the forest..." His voice trailed off.

The next day, the tragic news reached Dinakar that Tamilarasan had committed suicide by hanging.

"Gone. If he is alive, he will give some more trouble."

Dinakar was cruelly satisfied.

Next week, one morning, when Dinakar said "start" at a good time, the machines started moving slowly to clear the forest.

Dinakar had a triumphant smile on his face.

Suddenly the assistant came and said. "Sir...calling you from Chennai..."

Dinakar's wife spoke on the phone.

"What's the matter?" Dinakar asked, and there was silence for a few seconds at the other end. Then the wife said in a hoarse voice.

"Our boy has been sick for a week. He was suffering from stomach pain..."

"Did you take him to doctor...?"

"Yes....Take to doctor..." She stopped halfway...

Dinakar asked hurriedly. "What did the doctor say?"

"The doctor ran all the tests. Then..."

"Then what happened...?"

"Doctor said... our boy..."

" Our boy...?"

"Has cancer..."

The receiver slipped from Dinakar's hand.

He looked back suddenly. Giant machines were marching forward mercilessly cutting trees, plants and vines.

****

14. FACEBOOK FRIEND

Kathir Nilesh, who was turning twenty-seven that day, was very busy. There were many congratulatory messages for him on Facebook, Instagram and WhatsApp. He sat in his room after drinking tea at 8 in the morning and did not get up till 12 noon and was thanking those who sent him greetings. Even though father Mudhalmozhiyan and mother Malarvizhi came twice and called him. "I'm coming..." he gestured and kept running without getting up.

His father had retired from working as a teacher last year. His grandfather, who died five years ago, was very knowledgeable in Tamil. He named all his children in pure Tamil. One day when father Mudhalmozhiyan was talking to him he told him about his name. "Tamil appeared first among world languages. Your grandfather gave me this name to express it..." when he said "Oh...so..." he asked casually.

Mudhalmozhiyan was also engaged in literary work while working as an teacher. He has spoken on many platforms such as seminars, poetry halls and forums and has also written and published a collection of poems titled "Tomorrow is a Dream". But after the age of fifty-five he started to slow down and stay quiet at home. Reading books, watching TV and find a groom for his girl are the duties of him.

He named his son 'Kathir Nilavan'. When he changed it to Kathir Nilesh, Malarvizhi calmed him down. She told him that she and he had been talking two months ago. "He asked his mother if he was sorry.. Maa, why father has selected such an old model name for me...I said...Sun and moon have the qualities of both. That is, I told you that your father will give you this name in the meaning of heat and cold...But he said that he was going to change his name to take pride in it...Then last week he said...After changing his name to Kathir Nilesh, he would have got a lot of contacts on social media..."Mudhalmozhiyan looked at his wife in agony and left. Then as the days went by his anger subsided little by little and he too reluctantly accepted the name Kathir Nilesh.

Mudhalmozhiyan breathed a sigh of relief only when his daughter got married a year ago. As Kathir Nilesh was unemployed at that time, he could not help his father financially for his sister's wedding. Mudhalmozhiyan stood alone and tried hard to conduct the wedding well.

And then Kathir Nilesh joined in a unpopular I.T. company, got a modest salary. He was in touch with many friends on social media. When others sang his praises, his heart was very happy and he would say to his mother at home, "See...I am proud to be..." and he would become celebrated. When she told this to Mudhalmozhiyan, he satisfied that somehow son is famous in some way.

As it was past 12.30 p.m., Mudhalmozhiyan and Malarvizhi entered Kathir Nilesh's room and forced him to turn off his cell phone and laptop. Malarvizhi "Kathir... eat tiffin and come to talk... stomach is going to get bad..." Saying that, she took his hand and made him sit on the dining table. She put two idlis and dosa on the plate and poured some chutney and sambar and asked him to eat. Then she said "I will go upstairs and dry the clothes..." and went upstairs. Mudhalmozhiyan said to Kathir Nilesh, "After eating, take a five minute rest and then talk..." and went into the bathroom to take a bath.

The next second he finished eating the tiffin, the calling bell rang. He got up and opened the door. His Facebook friend Balaguru was standing there. Balaguru is a resident of Canada. Never met him in person except chat on Facebook. But his posts and photos are always different. So

Kathir Nilesh was able to recognize him immediately. In the morning he had wished Kathir Nilesh on his Facebook on his birthday. Suddenly he was surprised to see him but without revealing it, he asked questions like "Welcome Balaguru...when did you come from Canada...how did you find my address...".

Balaguru was surprised and asked Kathir Nilesh. "Is this your house...?"

"Yes..." said Kathir Nilesh with a smile.

"The home of the Poet Mudhalmozhiyan...?"

"He is my father...have you come to see him...?"

Balaguru smiled and looked at him with a creepy thought. "Yes...at the same time I am very happy to hear that you are his son..." he said.

"Get inside...father is in the bathroom...come now..." Kathir Nilesh brought Balaguru and made him sit on the sofa.

When Malarvizhi, coming down from the up floor after drying her clothes saw Balaguru and asked, "Hi...You are Kathir's friend...?".

Balaguru said "Yes Madam...". "She is mother..." when Kathir Nilesh said, Balaguru stood up and saluted Malarvizhi.

"Sit down...what to eat...coffee, tea, cool drinks...?" When mother asked, "Mother...I have just eaten five minutes ago...sit down...I have come to see sir..but I got pleasant surprise when I heard Kathir is his son...". Malarvigli understood that he had come to see her husband.

After bathing and wiping his head with a towel, Mudhalmozhiyan saw Balaguru and smiled a little and tried to go to his room. Balaguru suddenly stood up. Kathir Nilesh told his father that Balaguru had come to see him. He was a little surprised and said, "So....Brother, sit down..." He went into the room and put on his shirt and quickly came and sat on the sofa.

"Brother who are you...where are you from..." On hearing that, Balaguru told about himself and that he was Kathir Nilesh's Facebook friend and started telling the reason why he had come to see him.

"A month ago a website published an article about some poets titled "Rare Tamil Poets"...and they mentioned you too...They had taken two poems from your poetry book 'Tomorrow is a Dream'...When I read it, I was shocked..." Balaguru stopped, Kathir Nilesh and Malarvizhi looked at him in amazement. Muthalmozhiyan spoke to Balaguru quietly. "I wrote that book thirty years ago...If you say that the poems in it have attracted you...I am truly satisfied...Thank you!"

"Sir... I want to thank you... Nowadays, all modern poets write in such a way that even the readers cannot understand them...but thirty years ago you have written in a modern way and also that the readers can understand...how is this possible for you...?

"Brother...my father was a great scholar...but to tell you the truth, I got interested in Tamil only when I was twenty-five years old...all I studied was science, mathematics and economics...father one day told me a topic and said 'write poetry'. As a courtesy, I also tried to write a ten-line poem and showed it to him...He said "Good". I don't know that he sent it to the magazine. There was a big response for that poem from reader and I received a good remuneration. Apart from that I wrote one or two... I put everything together as a book... I did only one book... that's all..."

"Sir... Thiruvalluvar, Elango even these Poets have written only one book..." Mudhalmozhiyan looked up Balaguru and said, "Brother...how great they all are...you should talk to me along with them..."

"No...I meant to say that the number doesn't matter... real matter is what we write and that's the thing..."Balaguru spoke humbly.

"You are thinking well, brother..." said Muthalmozhiyan.

"Sir...your poetry book is different from other poetry books...have you thought about this?"

"There are three important things in poetry... they are form, content and sense. Most persons come to write poetry without knowing about it...when they say something new or deep, they think it is poetry.. That is, they decide that the content alone is enough... but a concept becomes a poem when the form and sense are also combined..."

Balaguru said, "Great...!". He continued "I found the name of the publishing house through net that published your book. I went there as soon as yesterday came to Chennai. They said that they don't have a single copy of your book... Then I asked them for your address, got it and came to see you..." he said.

"Yes brother...they print just one edition and leave it"

"I want a copy of your book. Is it available..." asked Balaguru curiously, Mudhalmozhiyan looked at him helplessly. "Somebody have bought all the books...now there is nothing..."

"Sir..Can you see and tell me if there is only one copy..." Balaguru asked without letting go. His great curiosity made him to think. "There are all the books I have read above Shelve.... if there is something mixed in there, you are lucky..."When he said that, Balaguru with renewed enthusiasm said, "Thank you...don't you want me to come and look for you...?" He asked.

"Don't do that...just talk for ten minutes...I'll see..." He got up and left. Kathir Nilesh was watching everything happening with a kind of new experience.

When he returned after a while Balaguru stood up expectantly. He said, "It's surprising... there were two copies of my book above.. I am thinking of the success of your interest..." He said to him, he bought the book, looked at his eyes and said, "Thank you...". "It's okay, brother...sit down..." said Mudhalmozhiyan.

"Sir.. Next month there will be a literature festival in Canada on behalf of the Tamil Sangam... Tamil scholars will speak on many topics... would you like to come there to speak on the topic of 'Poetry'... I am the treasurer of the Sangam...I have been telling my friends that I am coming anyway after talking to you..." Balaguru said with confidence.

"Brother...I can't come all that far..." he said, "Sir... we would be proud if you come.. You, mother and Kathir Nilesh should come. I will take care of you without any difficulty...I will make sure that there is no problem there..." he insisted with love.

Mudhalmozhiyan looked at Malarvizhi without replying, Malarvizhi looked at Kathir Nilesh. Balakularu spoke to Kathir Nilesh. "Kathiir...it's your responsibility to pick up father and mother in the plane...I expect you as my friend to do this..."

Kathir Nilesh thought for a while and said "Mother and father have never gone to any foreign country...why don't they board the plane...you say this is a good program...so I will bring them..."Saying that, Balaguru said "Thank you very much" and got up.

"Sir...You and mother stand together..." Balaguru requested and both of them stand up without understanding.

Balaguru suddenly bent down his head and touched their feet by hands for wishes.

"Brother...Brother...What's all this...be well..." Mudhalmozhiyan got him up.

After Balaguru had left happily, Kathir Nilesh alias Kathir Nilavan, looked humbly at his father, who was sitting on the sofa.

****

15. THE RIGHT PERSON

Shanmugam, who works at Auwai Aged Home, was at his home after taking leave for three days. His mind was filled with sadness.

Punitavathi had died before oneday who stayed in that home. Even though there were many elders, she had immense affection on him and he for her. One day his colleague Kumar said to him "Hi...you take care on her as your own grand mother". Shanmugam said "I don't know why it is happening...but I get satisfaction just by doing work for her..."

One day five years ago, someone picked her up in an auto and said to manager of home, "She layed in fainting at the beach...I read about your home in the paper...that's why I brought her here..." and left. Doctor, who came to the home by chance that day after examining her and told that she was very tired, was loaded with two bottles of glucose. She opened her eyes and asked Shanmugam who was standing there.

"Brother...where am I...?" He said, "Grandma, you are at Auwai's home..." From that day he used to talk to him affectionately. He also helped her without fail.

Someone would visit the elderly people staying there and pay a certain amount to the manager of the home. But no one comes to see Punitavathi. The manager one day asked her "What...how long will we help you...?" To say that, Punitavathi said "Should I leave from here..." Then Shanmugam spoke to the manager and resolved the problem and asked her to stay there. Many people are criticizing him as "You do service with pain for moneyless puppets..." He did helps to her as usual without hearing and caring other's comments.

She developed a personal affection for him because of an incident that happened one day.

That afternoon Shanmugam finished all the work and sat down to eat. He would have eaten only one mouthful.

"Oh, hungry... hungry..." Hearing the loud voice of Punitavathi, he got up from his meal and went to look. The old man who was there said sadly. "She got up to wash her hands...a dog came from somewhere and ate all the food of her..."

At that time there was no food in the home...If you want to buy food, you have to go to a hotel four kilometers away. Punitavathi was saying pitifully, "I'm hungry...I'm hungry..." Shanmugam rushed to bring his food and put it in front of her saying "Eat Grandma..." She finished eating everything in a hurry. She said to Shanmugam "Thank you very much..." "It's okay grandma..." he said and turned around.

He remembered that he had left home without eating anything because it was late in the morning. Hunger pinched his stomach as he hadn't eaten in the afternoon also. He was still walking with hunger. Had biscuits and tea in the evening. But the stomach has become somewhat artificial. When he went home at night, he could not eat. At home he said he was not feeling well and went to bed after eating only two dosas.

When he woke up the next day, stomach was somewhat better. It took two days for everything to return to normal.

A few days after Punitavathi called and spoke to him. "On that day what you gave me is your food...", he said "let it go grandma...". "Sinner.. you had given me everything and was starving..." she said with dismay.

One day Punitavathi noticed that Shanmugam was suffering from a shriveled face. "Shanmugam...it looks like something is bothering you... There is a suffice on your face..." she asked. Shanmugam said "Grandma... nothing..." But she asked again with persuasion, he said, "Grandma...I like a girl...I've been following her for a year...but she doesn't want to say a word..."

She told "Oh...Is this the matter...?" and then she recited a song written by Auvaiyar. "Do you know what this means...?" she asked him and said "No matter how hard we call out, what is not suitable for us will not come to us...at the same time, what is suitable for us will not leave us no matter how much we push it away..." He smiled thoughtfully.

One day Shanmugam approached Punitavathi to inquire about her family, and she spoke in desperation. "We are a fairly comfortable family...we have two boys. Both of them are well educated...the elder one has gone to Germany to find a job. He married a Tamil girl there. Another went to Norway.   He is with a white woman...seven years ago, when my husband died, the elder attened from Germany. He sent money for a while...then stopped it... Am I not a self-respecting person...I don't ask him for money... but he didn't think about what his mother would do...I sold our house and lived by that money. The money was melting little by little...One day I was sitting on the beach with worry...and fainted. A unknown good man brought me here..."Shanmugam's eyes were wet and he said, "Grandma...you have come here, don't worry anymore." She patted his cheek affectionately with her hand and expressed her love and gratitude.

Shanmugam saw Punitavathi who was walking slowly without health two weeks ago, "What's up Grandma...are you taking pills and medicine properly...?" She asked him to come near to her. She asked him in a slightly hoarse voice "I have a wish...can you fulfil it...?" He said, "Tell me grandmother...if I can, I will definitely do it."

She said "If I die, you do cremate me..."He suddenly covered her mouth and said, "Grandma, don't talk like that...you will be a hundred years old..."

But when she died the very next week, he could not stop crying. He has seen the death of many people staying in that home. They never affected him. But Punitavathi's death alone disturbed him. When he asked the manager of the house if he wanted to cremate her, he said, "We don't want this kind of new procedure." But after pleading with him for a long time and getting his permission, he fulfilled Punitavathi's last wish and stayed at house after taking leave for three days.

Suddenly, he heard a voice calling "Shanmugam...Shanmugam..." from the door, he came outside and looked. Kumar, who works with him in the home, was standing there.

"The manager asked you to come."

"What's the matter...?" Shanmugam asked hurriedly, "I don't know... I had come to the market. The manager called me and told that you just go and bring Shanmugam at once...," said Kumar.

Not understanding why the manager asked him to come, Shanmugam left with Kumar.

When they reached the home and entered the office there was a tall man sitting with the manager.

Manager said "Come on Shanmugam...Sir is Advocate Elangovan...He is waiting for you..."

Shanmugam greeted him. He also said hello and spoke patiently. "I am Punitavathi Ammal's family lawyer. Our father and his family are close friends. It was like I was staying in Mumbai for more than a year because of important work..

Also, I was not able to contact her as her phone number has changed...When I came to Chennai I went to see her. I had the news that she sold the house and left. Neighbors told me...she called them once and told that she was here and don't tell anyone about this and she told them if I come there, to ask me to meet her.

I came here one month ago to see her. You were on leave on that day. Punitavathi wrote her will and gave it to me. She told strictly to open the will after her death. I came here today by chance to see her. Unfortunately I heard about her demise.

When I opened the will, I found that she had written that the house at Kodaikanal belonging to her husband and the twenty sawaran of jewelery in the bank locker should go to you after her death" When he said that, Shanmugam was standing in tears.

The lawyer continued. " It's an old house. But today I think it's worth more than one crore... Bank has 20 Sawaran jewels..I will finish all the documents in the next two days...O.K..." Shanmugam was standing there not knowing what to say.

After talking for a while, the lawyer left. As he was walking towards the gate, Shanmugam got up with a thought and ran towards him. Seeing him, lawyer asked "What...what is...", "It has come sir..." He pulled back, "Shanmugam...if you want, I will arrange to sell the Kodaikanal house...I will also arrange to sell the jewelry to the right network which kept in the locker...not only that, I will make for a best deposit in your name in a good manner..." he said.

"It would be better if all are converted into cash. But I am not going to use that money for myself... My wish is to start a trust in her name and help the needy... You should guide me for that Sir..."when Shanmugam told the lawyer looked at him in surprise. He shooked hand with him happily.

Then with a smile he said "Shanmugam... don't worry...I will guide you!".

****

16. CULTURE

BBC titled "Tourist Guide Kalyani". Kalyani was very happy when she read a news article about her on the website, praising her excellent service. Travelers from different countries who came to Tamilnadu also had comments about Kalyani.

When Kalyani, now in her fifties, wanted to apply for this guide job twenty years ago, none of her husband's relatives agreed. She argued hard with them and won and applied for this job. Kalyani still remembers that when Kalyani told her father that she wanted to join this job, he praised her saying, "Very good...you should be able to speak English well for a guide job. You are an MA in literature. You can speak fluently. You have selected the right job...". After joining the job, Kalyani's interest in it and the way she interacted with tourists from abroad had earned her a good reputation.

When Kalyani came to the office that day, the manager told her about the tourists coming in the next two days. "England and France, ten people from these two countries are coming. They are going to visit the whole of Tamil Nadu.

It is your responsibility to spend two days only in the Chennai, suburbs and show them...I think you will manage as you know some French....hmm...good luck ma'am. "O.K..." Kalyani happily nodded.

Five of the tourists were male and five were female. One man and one woman are above fifty years of age.

Others are young. They set off in a large traveler van, chattering enthusiastically to infect Kalyani with their dynamism. Among them was Margaret Stella, a young woman who spoke with authority to Kalyani. "How many children do you have...?" Kalyani said, "Only girl...studying in college..." "I can't believe you're fifty, ma'am... you look like a thirty-five-year-old..."When she said that, Kalyani asked "Is it really true...?" She laughed.

Kalyani said, "We are going to see the Marina Beach first... It is the second longest beach in the World".

All got down in the beach and looked around there with joy for more than one hour. They willingly bought and ate the Pineapples and Cucumbers that were being sold at beach.

Then Kalyani announced, "Next we'll go to Pulicat Lake". Everyone nodded happily.

Sitting next to Kalyani in the van, Stella asked her some odd questions to fall into her ear. The questions were mostly about sex. "Will I answer all this later... " said Kalyani.

Kalyani noticed that all the passengers had a flood of happiness on their faces when they sailed the boat in Pulicat Lake.

They finished their lunch there and left for Kanchipuram. By the time they returned to Chennai after visiting the important temples and silk production sites in Kanchipuram, it was almost ten o'clock at night. Kalyani brought them to the pre-booked hotel and left them saying "We will leave tomorrow morning at 9...Everyone get ready ok...good night..." he said and left for home.

Kalyani laughed thoughtfully as she remembered the questions asked by Stella, the girl from France, after going home.

They left the next morning and went to Mahabalipuram and Vedantangal. Kalyani's description of Mahabalipuram including the history of the Pallavas greatly impressed the travellers. Next, they saw many kinds of birds in Vedantangal and captured them on camera without letting go of everything. After leaving there and reaching Valluvar Kottam in Chennai at six o'clock in the evening, everyone's eyes widened when Kalyani told about the excellence of Thirukkural and that it has been translated into many languages in the world.

While everyone else was looking around Valluvar Kottam, only Stella was sitting alone talking to someone on her cell phone. Kalyani went near her and waited for her to finish speaking and then smiled. She sat next to her and started talking friendly. She politely answered her questions that are asked for two days. She answered some of them in a leafy way. Then he asked her "Where did you get so many sexual suspicions...May I know the reason for that...?

"Ma'am...I'm getting married next month...you are older...you have a lot of experience...that's what I asked..." said Stella.

"Ohh...that's the thing...Congrats..." when Kalyani told, Stella smiled and thanked her.

She asked Kalyani "Madam...how many years have you been married...?".

"It's been twenty years..." said Kalyani. A look of surprise crossed Stella's face.

"Wow... twenty years... doesn't living with someone for so many years get you bored..." Stella asked, Kalyani thought with a bit of shock.

"Utter boring..." She suppressed the words that came to her mouth and said "No... no... it's our culture...!

****

17. WHO

The "Discussion Stage" program aired on the popular T.V. channel "Vaimai" has received overwhelming response from the audience. This is telecasted every Sunday of the week at night from 8 to 9 o' clock. In this program various subjects are analysed. People from various departments will also participate. The host of the show, Arivumani knows all things according to his name.

Such an important debate forum had reached its hundredth week. As it was the hundredth week, people had a lot of expectations. The program usually concludes with discussions. But since it is the hundredth week, it was also announced that 'the verdict' will be given at the end of the show. With all this in mind, the week asked, "Who are largely responsible for the country's problems - People or Politicians?" The title was given.

The shooting of the 100th weekly show, which to be telecasted after two days, began at a stage, located in the city's main studio. It was attended by ruling party person Manivannan, opposition party speaker Fire Natarajan, Journalist Vivekanandan, Social activist Pandian and sixty people in the audience.

The host of the show, Arivumani briefed everyone and explained the topic once again.

"Sometimes problems arise in the country due to the decisions of politicians. Sometimes created by people. But today's debate is about who is to blame highly. I request them to take this into consideration and give their views."

Those who had come as spectators spoke admirably of various opinions. Then Arivumani invited those who came as special invitees to speak. "Journalist Vivekanandan will give his views first" he handed him the mic.

Vivekanandan delivered his views in a shrill voice. "People vote and elect the rulers. Many times the people who have voted, the rulers are behaving in such a way that the people who have voted are upset and say, 'Why did we vote for them?'

Sometimes people say ``Aha'' but after a while the old pattern comes back. This means that people are still dissatisfied with the rulers.

Most of the time Politicians fail to fulfil their promises to the people during elections. Many reasons are given for this. At this point we have to blame the people.

People don't think about the promises made by politicians. Let us bend the sky; Despite the promises that we will turn the sand into hay, the people believe and cast their vote and are left behind. Therefore, according to me, both the people and the politicians are equally responsible for the country's problems." Loud applause arose from the audience.

Manivannan, the ruling party leader, cleared his throat and began to make his point. "Government is like walking on a tight rope in up. Everyone should be thankful to the politicians who manage everything on their heads. A game can be freely and happily enjoyed by the audience. But only the players standing on the field know the pain and suffering. They accept it for fame. In the same way politicians also lead a sacrificial life for the sake of the country." A certain amount of applause arose when he said this.

Next, Aruvumani gave the microphone to the opposition speaker Fire Natarajan, who straightened the towel on his shoulder and started speaking. "Politics has been researched since the time of Aristotle. A politician works for the country all his life. However, the society labels him as selfish. A politician standing in the field bearing blows and insults shows his good spirit and character of service. It cannot be denied that some weeds grow in the world of politics. We need to get rid of them and it is unacceptable to blame the politicians for the problems of the country as a whole."

Many times, Manivannan and Fire Natarajan, who often clashed fiercely, gave almost the same opinion which surprised the audience.

Next social activist Pandian was given an opportunity to speak.

Applause erupted even before he spoke as he was a celebrity who had participated in many events. Pandian made his point in a calm yet emphatic manner. Manivannan and Natarajan looked at him with angry faces when he said, "Surely the country's problems are largely due to the politicians." He continued his speech without worrying about anyone. "People elect a politician who has 100 percent faith. But when a politician comes to power, even ten percent of the faith of people don't behave like they are trusted...when the people realize that they have been cheated, the next election comes. People choose someone else next time...He is also behaving in the same way," he said and got a huge round of applause.

Manivannan interrupted in the middle. "Does a politician jumps from the sky...he comes from the people..." he concluded. Pandian gave the right answer to that.

"Politicians come from the people. I agree... But when he come to power, he forgets the people. Apart from thinking how to uplift himself and his family in the economy, he forgets how to improve the economic condition of the country and what plans can be made for the poor and needy people. An honest politician can surely take the country on the path of progress...but there are no such politicians today...that's why politicians are the main cause of the country's problems..."When Pandian spoke, applause and cheers shook the hall.

Arivumani announced, "Tea break for half an hour...go outside and come back as soon as you can..." and when he left to go to the washroom, the assistant came and whispered in his ear. "Sir...MD has come...he is sitting in the room. He told me to come and see you right away."

Arivumani was surprised. MD Ramnath is a very busy man. He never comes to the shooting site. He doesn't understand why he came today and wanted to talk to him.

When fastly Arivumani entered the room, M.D. greeted him with a smile, "Come on, Mr. Arivumani..." and asked him to sit on the chair in front of him.

He spoke a little nervously. "Are you going to give your verdict on today's debate platform...?" he asked.

"Yes sir..." he said and M.D. felt with a sigh of relief.

"I ran here to talk about an important matter... An hour ago, Minister Karmukilan came to our T.V. office.... He asked me what judgment would give in today's discussion forum...I told him that the judgment will be decided by Host Arivumani. But he retorted a lot and told me to judge because the people are the cause..."

Arivumani suddenly asked. "How can he interfere with our freedom sir...we will have to give judgment no matter what we want...did you tell him this sir..?"

"Arivumani...what you say is correct...but our TV's situation...we were in the second place and have progressed little by little and reached the first place ..Karmukilan's party is going to rule for another four years...surely we will need the support of the government...if we behave as he says....he indirectly telling us that we are getting support from them..."

"Sir...I have always conducted this program through neutrality..."

"Yes...yes...I know very well about your talent and honesty...This is a difficult situation for us...if you just give judgment like he said it will be good for everyone...I think you understand what I am saying..."

Arivumani was sitting with his head bowed without answering. M. D. he asked with a pat on the shoulder. "Have I ever interfered in your program, Arivumani?".

Arivumani slowly looked up at him. "Do as I said just this one time...O.K..." said MD and Arivumani intervened half-heartedly.

****

18. TURNINGS

Amudhan, who was waiting for Kavitha in the park, sat up straitly when he saw her coming from a short distance away.

Her face was some dull perspective which always had a smile.

Kavitha sat near Amudhan and wiped her face with the head of her saree.

"Why is a strange mood with you today..." Amudhan asked,

She said "nothing...a dilemma in the office...that's the way the mind is..."

"What's up Kavitha... is there any problem" Amudhan asked in a slightly worried voice.

"Do you remember that which I told you last week about the son of our company boss who has arrived from America..."

"Yes...I remember even saying his name is Madan..."

"Correct...he came to the office today and talked to me for a while...he said 'I like you' when he left. Shocked Amudhan asked after thinking for a while.

"He would have appreciated your skill at work..."

"I thought so too. But when he left, he smiled at me in a different way... It felt like..."

"Hm... then you should be a little careful with that person..."

"That's what I thought."

Suddenly Kavitha started coughing. She continued to cough, Amudhan said, "Kavitha...drink water..."

She took the bottle from her hand bag and drank water and gave it to Amudhan.

He drank a little and gave it back. She coughed again and struggled to stifle it.

"Have you taken any medicine..." Kavitha motioned to him asking him to be patient.

"I have had a cough for a week. I have never had such a continuous cough. I took medicine. But it won't go away. The doctor I usually go for treatment has gone to Mumbai...he will come tomorrow..."

"Definitely see the doctor..."

"Hm..."

The branches of trees in the park began to move slowly. The wind started blowing. Both of them sat without talking for a while

"Mm...is any information about the interview you went last month..." Kavitha asked him expectantly.

"Look Kavitha...I forgot to tell you...I just received a letter saying that I was not selected as usual..."

"Hmm... The interview was all a hoot... what do you say..."

"You are right...but what is another way..." Amudhan said in a relaxed voice.

After some time they left there, went to the nearby shop, had biscuits and tea and came to the bus stop.

"Mm... don't talk too much with that Madan...ok..."starring Kavitha, Amudhan said that, when she was shaking her head the bus had arrived and she got in. She waved hand to him from the bus, he also waved.

He was standing there thinking for a while as the bus was leaving, he boarded the Share auto and left for home.

Kavitha works as a clerk in a Private Concern. An elderly father, mother and a slightly disabled younger sister are responsible for saving them.

Amudhan is an unemployed graduate. His father is a retired middle school teacher. The family runs on the father's pension money.

Amudhan's desire is to accept the burden of the family. He is trying to get a job by sending applications to many places. Amudhan and Kavitha, who met at a bus stand, became lovers within a few months. Their bonding continues for more than two years. Now Madankumar, the son of the boss of the company where Kavitha works, has come as a villain for their love.

A few days have passed. Kavitha stayed in her seat even past office hours as there was work that needed to be completed immediately. Madankumar suddenly came there. He spoke to her with pretension.

"Kavitha....didn't you go home...?"

"No sir...I have to finish some work...that's it..." Kavitha replied respectfully.

"I like your sincerity..."

"Thank you sir..."

"That's all right...by the bye...may I personally talk to you about a few things..."

"Sir...Personal matter in office..."

"Don't hesitate...It is a simple one..."

"O.K. Tell me sir..."

Madankumar relucted for a few seconds and then asked, "Hmm...have you decided anything about your marriage..."

"Why sir...why are you asking..."

"Just asking to know..."

"That's for parents to decide, sir..."

"Kavitha...I'll be frank...I want to marry you...May I know what you think..."

"Sir...what are you talking about..." Kavitha looked at him shocked.

"No tension please...You don't need to answer now... tell tomorrow or two or three days later...ok...I will come..."

Without waiting for her reply, Madankumar left quickly.

The next day Kavitha met Amudhan and told him what happened in the office.

He felt very angry.

"His money makes him talk like that... I will come to your office and see him and ask him what..."

"No... you don't come...if he come again...I will give the right answer and put an end to this problem. O.K..."

Amudhan looked at her face for a while and then said "Mm... Ok...".

Suddenly she coughed holding her stomach. She drank some water and relieved herself.

Amudhan asked her worriedly. "Did you see the doctor..."

"I forgot to tell you...Yesterday went and looked. He gave me an injection and prescribed a pill. He told me to come back after a week and see him again."

"Take pill without fail..."

"Alright..."

Kavitha was told by her father with a smile when she came home that evening.

"Your company boss came to our house..."

"Why did he come here..." Kavitha asked a bit shocked.

" Everything is good... he asked you to marry his son..."

"What did you say..."

"I said yes...as he said he will bear all the expenses of your sister's study and wedding expenses...I think you have no objection..."

"Could you have asked me a word..."

"The way he spoke was good...I also thought about our family situation.... that's why I said that..."

"Daddy...I hid something from you...forgive me...I like a person namely Amudhan..."

When Kavitha said this, her father, mother and younger sister looked at her in shock.

Mom asked urgently. "Kavitha...what you say..Will this be okay with our family..."

"He's a graduate...he's looking for a job...he'll get a job soon...besides that, he's getting married right away..."

There was silence for a while. Then Dad cleared his throat and spoke.

"Kavitha..I don't need to tell you...our family situation, Your sister's future is in your hands...some good luck has come to our home for us. It is not right to ignore it...you should think carefully and give your answer..

He looked up at Kavitha and suddenly went into the room.

Kavitha realized for the first time that a complicated situation had arisen in her life.

When she woke up the next day, her head felt a little heavy. The body was tired.

She called the office and asked for two days leave and came out of the room.

Dad was sitting on the chair with a worried face.

When he saw Kavitha asked "Why you are seen dull..."

"Nothing...a little headache..." She took the morning tea and put the pill and went to bed. She woke up at three in the afternoon. She felt that the headache and body ache had subsided.

Kavitha called Amudhan to tell him about her Boss' home visit, but her phone received a reply saying "Switch off". Usually Amudhan's cell phone is always on. She doesn't understand why it's off now.

Kavitha received a phone call from Amudhan at around 7 pm. She was relieved when he told Kavitha that he had to go to Chengalpattu with a relative from the town and that his phone had run out of charge. "I want to talk to you right away.. Are you coming to visit tomorrow..." asked Kavitha, "I will..." Amudhan said.

Next morning Kavitha's father told her "Dear... you don't say anything about your marriage matter...what will I say if your company boss asks anything further...I think your decision will support our family..."he said.

"Dad...I don't know how to answer you now...can we talk tomorrow..." she said and left to see Amudhan.

Shortly after Kavitha left, the boss called. Kavitha's father politely said "Hello sir...tell me...".

"Then.. Astrologer said. Within ten days a very auspicious day is coming...it's a very special day...I'm thinking of conduct a simple engagement...what do you think..."

Kavitha's father thought for a while. Then he summoned courage and said. "You senior, see and decide will be correct!"

"Good then... I will call you with the actual date and time..."

When the boss hung up the phone, Kavitha's father was afraid of what she would say. However, he made up his mind to talk to her somehow and get her to agree to the marriage.

Meeting Amudhan in the park, he was shocked when she told him that the situation had become very complicated.

"Kavitha...I will come to your house...I will tell your father that I love you..."

While he was talking to Kavitha, Madankumar suddenly came there.

"Kavitha...are you here...oh who is this..." Madan asked Kavita and she remained silent. Amudhan stared at Madan and asked Kavitha. "Who is this..."

Kavitha said slowly. "This is Madankumar"

Madankumar said to Amudhan with little annoyingly. "Mister...let it be that you are questioning me.... you need to know one thing. Me and Kavitha are going to get engaged next week. from now on, everything happening like this is wrong...please understand..." Then he said to Kavitha "I am leaving..." and left.

He asked her with a sudden idea. "Oh...why did you take leave to office..."

"Not feeling well..."

"Come on...let's go to the doctor..."

"No... I'm going to see the family doctor..."

"Ok ok...take care of the body. Leave now..."

Madankumar stared at Amudhan and left quickly.

Amudhan asked Kavitha in a panic. "What Kavitha... Is engagement..."

"I don't understand anything...I'll go home and call you..."

"Kavitha...I have no life without you..."

Kavitha was also disturbed by Amudhan's stammering.

"You leave...I will call you in the evening..." Without waiting for bus Kavitha hurriedly got a auto and came to home. She asked her father at once when she entered the house.

"Has the company boss come here...what did you say...I don't know what's going on..."

Mother and sister came out of the kitchen hearing Kavitha's voice. Dad spoke quietly to Kavitha.

"He spoke only on phone...the coming 20th is an auspicious day...he asked if he could make engagement event on that day?."

"What did you say..."

"Kavitha...Do you remember what I said to you two days ago.... I can't say no to anything as we have such family situation. I said ok..."

"So you don't care about my preferences...don't you..."

"Why are you talking like this...If you have a good life in a good place then we all will be happy...I took this decision after thinking carefully..."

"Even after I told you that I like someone, you did make this decision..."

"Kavitha...do you understand something...if there is no money in this world life will not go well...we may have many desires and wishes...but should we think about anything realistically...Not only your future but also our family's future lies in the decision you take..."

"Father, what will you do if I do not agree to this marriage..."

After a while Dad said firmly. "What can do... the three of us should commit suicide..."

Kavitha did not expect these words from her father. Even after this she could not speak against her father.

Tears suddenly began to well up in her eyes. Fastly she entered the room and fell on the bed.

Amudhan was disturbed when he did not receive any information from Kavitha who said that she would call him in the evening.

He had the idea of visiting Kavitha at her house but he hesitated as to how to go there without her permission.

Amudhan could not sleep that night.

After two o'clock he fell on sleep but suddenly at three o'clock he woke up and sat on the bed.

'Perhaps Kavitha would have agreed to the marriage'

Doubt arose in his mind and he got off the bed and started pacing into his room.

His father got up to pee and accidentally saw Vasanthan walking into the room and came in "What's up...?" he asked.

Amudhan said "Nothing..." But father asked him that again.

"When I watching you, it's seem like you're in trouble, whatever it is, tell me obviously..."

Amudhan did not want to hide his love affair from him anymore. He told him everything that happened while looking at the ground.

Contrary to Amudhan's thought that father was going to scold him on hearing this, he spoke with love.

"Dear...why didn't you tell me this earlier..."

Amudhan was silent to hear him.

He continued. "Love is a different thing in this world. The percentage of people who win it is very less. But you should understand that love is not the only thing in life.. Relax and sleep... Everything will be fine..." After hearing his father's comforting words, his mind calmed down a bit.

Waking up the next morning, Amudhan's thoughts were dominated by the memory of Kavitha every second. After some thinking he called her.

Kavitha's father spoke on the other end. "Brother... Kavita has told about you...she is going to get married. She is feeling a little sick now...Don't call her anymore..."

"Has she seen the doctor..." Amudhan asked with concern.

"Yesterday she met the doctor...he has given her medicine... she is sleeping peacefully now...Don't disturb her anymore. She has a good tide up...We have a good time for our family too...Don't spoil everything...please...I am ready to come and fall at your feet...please forget her..." he begged in a hoarse voice.

Amudhan hung up the phone without answering. He stood in thought for a while and wiped the rising water from his eyes.

The whole day he thought about many things. Eventually he came to the conclusion of trying to forget Kavitha.

About two weeks have passed. Amudhan was standing at the bus stop. When a female employee working in Kavitha's office saw him, she came near him and spoke with a sad face.

"Sir, do you know the matter...Kavitha resigned her job...and the marriage has also stopped..."

Amudhan asked hurriedly "Why...what did happen...?"

"I don't know the reason sir...the bus has arrived for me... I get leave..." she said and got on the bus.

Amudhan was shocked. He came home and spoke to his father. He and father went to Kavitha's home.

When they reached Kavitha's house, the house was quiet. Amudhan peeked inside.

Kavitha was sitting in a chair. Her father lay on the easel with troubled eyes. Her mother and younger sister sat quietly on the floor.

"Kavitha..."When Amudhan looked up to speak, Kavitha got up from the chair and invited, "Come... Come in..." Seeing Amudhan and his father, Kavitha's father, mother and younger sister stood up with a question mark, not knowing who they were.

"Dad...this is Amudhan and he is his father..." Kavitha introduced them both to her family.

"Sit..." Kavitha's father covered his mouth with his hand and start to sob.

"Kavitha...what happened..." asked Amudhan, Kavitha remained silent.

Kavitha's father spoke soothing voice "A week ago, Kavitha went to the doctor for the test...Unbeknownst to her, that Madankumar went to the hospital and inquired. The next day his father came and told that the engagement of his boy and Kavitha was cancelled..."

"What's wrong with Kavitha's body...please tell me..."

After a moment of silence Kavitha's father said in a choked voice. "Brother...Kavitha has congenital heart disease...it's an incurable disease..."

Amudhan felt as if thunder had fallen on his head. Amudhan's father looked at his son in shock. Amudhan sat leaned on the chair. For a while he closed his eyes and sat with his head bowed in thought. Kavitha's father's sob was joined by her mother and sister's little cry.

Amudhan slowly straightened up and spoke to Kavitha's father.

"Sir...Kavitha and I really loved each other sincerely... but fate played Madan's role...I was shocked when Kavitha was asked to marry him...Then I thought about your family situation...After you talked to me on the phone, my mind became a little clearer... Kavitha has a comfortable life... I made up my mind that she should be well..."

Kavitha looked at Amudhan with troubled eyes. He continued to speak.

"This morning at the bus stop, I saw a lady who works in Kavitha's office. From her statement, I understood that there is something wrong with your house...I immediately brought my father and come here."

Amudhan looked at everyone for a few seconds and continued in a firm voice

"Sir.. my love was not based on just looks...I loved Kavitha's heart...now that she has a heart disease, this news does not diminish my love for her at all...to tell you the truth...now I love Kavitha more...I am ready to marry her the minute if you give your consent..."

Kavitha's father, who was listening to Amudhan's speech with wide eyes, looked at him with gratitude.

"Brother...I did mistakes without understanding the true love that you have for Kavitha...as a punishment for that, our family has suffered such a great shame...if I act without conscience after this, I am not a human being...Hmm....As you say that you are willing to marry her on purpose, I also whole heartedly agree... Our girl is very lucky..."

Kavitha's father said with emotion.

Kavitha tried to say something, father told her to be quiet, he went near to Amudhan's father.

"Sir.. You are elder, don't say anything yet..."

He asked holding his hand.

Amudhan's father kindly told him. "Whatever decision my son takes, it must be honest and humane...so I will not block any action with him...I fully agree with this marriage..."

Suddenly they heard a car sound at the door. Everyone turned their gaze towards the door. Kavita's family doctor got out of the car and was coming fast.

Kavitha and Dad looked at each other not understanding why the doctor was coming home. Kavitha told Amudhan.

"He is our family doctor..."

"Is this the one who took the test for you..." Amudhan asked, she nodded 'yes'.

As soon as the doctor came into the house, Kavitha's father said, "Come on Sir ...please be seated..."said that in a respectful tone, the doctor looked at everyone and spoke hurriedly.

"First I apologize to all of you...I'm so sorry..."

"Doctor...what wrong did you do to apologize..." Kavitha's father asked without understanding.

"I didn't make a mistake...my Assistant made a mistake..."

"Sir...I don't understand what you are saying..."

"On the same day as our Kavitha came for checkup, another woman named Kavitha also came for treatment...Her report was typed as Kavitha's report by Assistant. I came to know about the mistake today when that woman arrived to get the report...that's why I ran immediately...I'm sorry...extremely sorry...Kavitha's body has no problem..."

Everyone looked at the doctor with a kind of happy shock.

"Doctor... tell me the truth... my girl is not sick at all..." Kavitha's father asked breathlessly.

"She's perfectly all right...there's no one healthier than her."

Doctor said a little louder,

Everyone looked at him with a smile of relief in their hearts.

The doctor told Kavitha. "Kavitha will you forgive me..."

"Sir... you elder...Don't go to ask me the forgiveness..." Kavitha said humbly.

"Doctor...this mistake you made saved Kavitha from a big danger..." When Kavitha's father told, the Doctor looked him without understanding.

"What do you mean...big risk...?"

Kavitha spoke to doctor as her Dad hesitated how to tell what had happened.

"Sir... Father had decided to make my marriage with the son of a millionaire. Thinking that I am ill, the man said that he will not marry me. That's what Dad says..."

"Oh...so many things happened...you didn't even say a word..."

"Sorry Sir...I don't like to talk about unwilling marriage Sir..."

"Ok...Ok...." the doctor looked at Amudhan and his father who are they and Kavitha's father introduced them to the doctor.

"Hello Sir..."Doctor wished at Amudhan's father and went to Amudhan and greeted him with a handshake.

After thanking him, Amudhan looked at Kavitha.

"Kavitha there is a glad tiding..."

"What..." Kavitha asked curiously.

"I have got a job in the public works department...just got the order..."

"So..." Kavitha looked at Amudhan with a pleasant surprise.

"Very good...very good..." the Doctor complimented him. Everyone congratulated Amudhan. The house was full of joy

******

About the Author

AR. Arul Selvan was born on 1961. He retired from India Post Department and resides with family in Chennai. He has been writing in Tamil more than 30 years. His writings were published in magazines, broadcasted through Radio and telecasted by Television. Books with collection of his Poems, Short stories, Articles and Plays have also been published.

Email: writerararulselvan@gmail.com